the blue songbird

vern kousky

RP | KIDS
PHILADELPHIA

Once, there lived a blue songbird.

Every morning she would wake up,
hop to the edge of a high branch,
and listen to her sisters' lovely songs.

The songbird always tried to join in
with them, but she could never sing
like they could sing.

"I'm not like
my older sisters,"
said the songbird
to her mother.
"It seems there
are no songs
for me."

"My dearest one,"
replied her mother,
"not just any notes will
do. You must go and
find a special song
that only you
can sing."

So the songbird left her mother, left her nest, and all she knew, and flew off to find her special song.

When she reached a far-off land,
she saw a giant bird, unlike any she'd
ever seen before.

The songbird landed and began
to chirp:

"Excuse me, Mr. Long-Necked Bird,
    in your travels have you heard
      of a very special thing—
        a song that only I can sing?"

The bird stretched
his slender neck
down low to where
the songbird stood.

"My name is Crane,"
whooped the bird,
"and I'm sorry
that I can't help you.
But see those
mountains over there?
Beyond them lives
the wisest bird.
If anyone knows
where to find the
answer, I'm sure it
will be him."

The songbird kindly
thanked the crane,
then flew off
to continue her quest.

She soared over the mountain peaks and dove down into a deep valley until she reached a dark pine forest.

Here she found a bird who looked old and very wise.

"Hello, Mr. Wise Old Bird.
   In your long life, you must have heard
      of a very special thing—
         a song that only I can sing."

"I am Owl," hooted the bird. "Whooooo are you
looking for?"

"No, not who," answered the songbird. "I'm searching
for a song!"

But the owl only cocked his head.
"Whoooo? Whoooo?"

This must not be the wise bird after all, thought the
songbird. Still, she thanked him kindly, then flew off
once more to continue her quest.

The songbird crossed rivers and valleys, cities and oceans.

All along the way, she always asked where she might find her song.

USE
ACME
SOAP

But no bird ever had the answer.

One windy winter day, she met a bird who looked a
little bit mean and more than a little bit hungry.
Even so the songbird bravely chirped:

"Please don't eat me, Mr. Scary Bird.
    I just wondered if you've ever heard
        of a very special thing—
            a song that only I can sing."

"Call me Crow," cawed the bird.
"And I *have* heard of such a thing.
Across the sea there is an island,
golden as the sun and filled with
the most enchanting music.
Fly west as far as you can, and there
you will find the song you seek."

The songbird kissed the clever crow,
then set out to cross the sea.

She flew through
storm and wind,
through night
and day, until she
was more tired
than she had ever
been. But the
songbird did not
rest, for she
knew that soon
she'd find her
special song.

Then
she saw the
island, glowing like
a jewel on the horizon.
In the distance, she could
hear the sound of beautiful music.

"At last! I made it!" laughed the
songbird, and suddenly her
wings felt strong again.
She swooped down,
faster and faster,
following the
sound,
until
she found,
that after all this time . . .

she was home.

The songbird's heart fell.
She had circled the whole world,
spoken to every bird there was,
but her quest had failed.

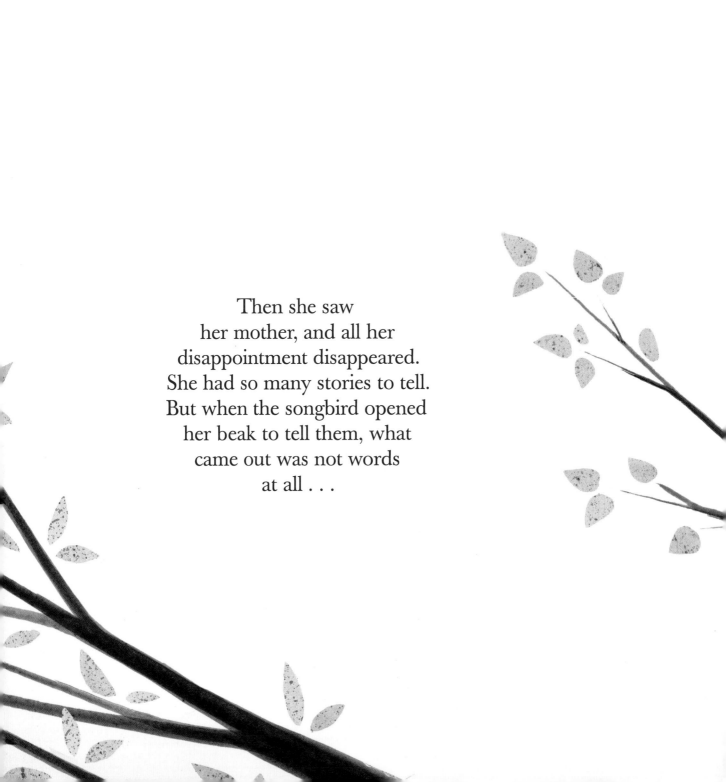

Then she saw
her mother, and all her
disappointment disappeared.
She had so many stories to tell.
But when the songbird opened
her beak to tell them, what
came out was not words
at all . . .

but a song!

She sang a song of Crane and Owl
and of the clever Crow,
of cities and of stormy seas
and mountains capped with snow,
of all the warm and sunny days
and the chilly nights alone,

and of the love the songbird felt
for her family and her home.